# » DANILO «
# the Fruit Man

*Amy Valens*

Dial Books for Young Readers  New York

Published by Dial Books for Young Readers
A Division of Penguin Books USA Inc.
375 Hudson Street · New York, New York 10014
Copyright © 1993 by Amy Valens / All rights reserved
Design by Sara Reynolds
Printed in Hong Kong by
South China Printing Company (1988) Limited
First Edition
1 3 5 7 9 10 8 6 4 2

Library of Congress Cataloging in Publication Data
Valens, Amy
Danilo the fruit man/story and pictures by Amy Valens.
p. cm.
Summary: Danilo, a fruit-seller in Sicily, leads a peaceful and
contented life until he finds unusual trees with magical fruit.
ISBN 0-8037-1151-4 (tr.) — ISBN 0-8037-1152-2 (lib.)
[1. Fruit — Fiction. 2. Peddlers and peddling — Fiction.
3. Magic — Fiction. 4. Sicily (Italy) — Fiction.]
I. Title.
PZ7.V227 Dan 1993
[E] — dc20 91-46893 CIP AC

The art was created with watercolors, colored tissue paper, and newspaper.
The borders were inspired by designs on traditional Sicilian horse carts.

## ITALIAN PRONUNCIATIONS

| | |
|---|---|
| *aperto* | ah-PEAR-toe |
| *arance fresche* | ah-RAHN-chay FRES-kay |
| *basta* | BAH-sta |
| *buon appetito* | bwun ah-pe-TEE-toe |
| *buon giorno* | bwun JOR-no |
| *carretta* | kar-RET-ta |
| *che tipo* | kay TEE-po |
| *Danilo* | dah-NEE-lo |
| *dolci* | DOL-chee |
| *finalmente* | fee-nal-MEN-tay |
| *frutta misteriosa* | FROO-ta mis-te-ree-O-sa |
| *grazie* | GRAHT-see-eh |
| *Ninicchio* | nee-NEE-kee-o |
| *nonna, nonno* | NO-na, NO-no |
| *pane e formaggio* | PAH-nay ay for-MAH-jee-o |
| *primo* | PREE-mo |
| *secondo* | se-KON-doe |
| *tarantella* | ta-rahn-TEL-a |

FOR VITO AND ROSARIA'S
GREAT-GRANDCHILDREN
KEJA, JESSE
NATASIA, JAZMIN
AND SAWYER

RICORDO
SICILIA

**D**anilo the fruit man lived on the island of Sicily, in a house surrounded by orange trees. He had five chickens to give him eggs, a green-eyed cat to chase mice, and a sturdy horse to pull his *carretta* — his cart. Every morning he filled the cart with ripe oranges, and rode to town.

Danilo walked up and down the narrow streets, calling, "Oranges — fresh oranges! *Arance — arance fresche!*"

People leaned out their windows when they heard his call, and when they saw the cheery cart filled with beautiful fruit, they would come down and buy some.

Danilo packed the oranges in newspaper cones that he'd made the night before. He knew all the streets of the town, and most of the people. With his jokes and stories Danilo could always make a child laugh or an old *nonna* smile.

When his *carretta* was empty, Danilo would tell himself, "Money in my pocket, oranges on my trees...life is good!" He would buy bread and cheese — *pane e formaggio* — and then ride home.

One hot day Danilo had walked through the whole town, and had sold almost all of his oranges. "Ah, Ninicchio," he said to his horse, "what more could I want?"

Just then Danilo saw a street he'd never noticed before.

"Eh!" he thought. "I must have passed this road a hundred times without seeing it!" Danilo turned up the steep hill, calling, *"Arance dolci!* Sweet oranges! *Arance fresche!"*

But no one came to the windows. The only answer to his cry echoed back from the cobblestones, *"Arance fresche . . ."*

The horse flicked his ears nervously. Danilo patted his old friend, saying, "Never mind, Ninicchio. There's nobody here, but at the top of the hill we'll have a fine view of the town! I think I see a park. Surely there will be people there on a day like today."

And when they reached the top they saw a sign that read
*Aperto* — Open. "A park, Ninicchio, just as I thought." There
were no sounds of children playing or people chatting, but
Danilo didn't notice.

He was staring at the trees — they were unlike any he'd ever seen. Purple, pink, and blue fruits covered them and were scattered all over the grass. The air was filled with their fragrance.

Danilo saw an old man sitting under one of the trees. "Good day to you, *nonno*," he said. *"Buon giorno!* Can you tell me…are these fruits good to eat?"

"Good to eat? Why just taste one, my friend. *Buon appetito!*"

Danilo took a bite. Ah! Could anything be so delicious? He tried a blue one, then a purple, then a pink. They tasted to him like the sunrise, and the sunset, and the first day of summer. Danilo laughed, and the wrinkly old man laughed too. Danilo sang, and the old man sang too. Soon they were dancing a *tarantella* all over the grass — hopping nimbly over the fruit, of course.

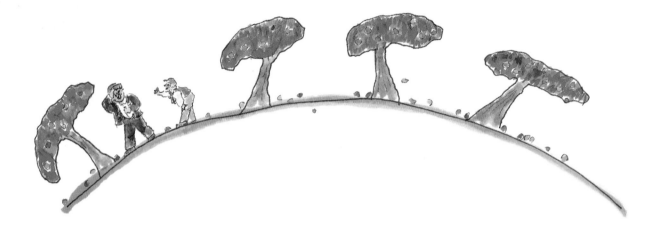

"*Basta* — Enough!" the old man said. "I haven't danced like that in a hundred years!"

"Oh, *nonno!*" Danilo cried. "This fruit…could I grow trees with such fruit?"

The old man scratched his chin. Then he sang in a trembly voice:

> *Primo, primo* — First, you must not need them
> *Secondo* — Second, they must be free
> *Finalmente*, you'll only grow them
> From a seed you cannot see!

Danilo fanned himself with his hat. "It's too hot to guess at riddles. Tell me, what's the answer?"

"Answers I can't give you . . . only fruit."

Danilo looked at all the fruit lying in the grass. "Will you help me load my cart?"

"With pleasure," the old man replied, and they worked together until the cart was full.

"*Grazie, nonno* — thank you!" Danilo said. "*Grazie.*"

The old man watched him go. "Remember the song, Danilo!" he called.

But Danilo didn't hear. He never even looked back. He was busy thinking, "I have so much fruit now, I can sell some, and still have plenty of seeds! And when they grow, I can rip out my orange trees, and have these instead! Just imagine how much money I'll make!"

When he came to a familiar street, Danilo called out, *"Frutta misteriosa!* Fantastic! Exquisite!"* Many curious people looked to see what mysterious fruit he was selling. But when they saw Danilo's cart, they all began to laugh.

"Danilo's lost his head! Who does he think will eat those?"

"No! no!" he cried. "Just taste them! They're delicious!"

And he turned to pick up some of the beautiful fruit.

Danilo gasped. His *carretta* was filled with rocks! "Who has taken my fruit and left me with this?" he shouted.

But the people just laughed and went back to their work, saying, "That Danilo! *Che tipo*—what a character!"

That night Danilo grumbled as he piled the rocks in his yard, "I'll go back tomorrow, and this time I'll keep an eye on that fruit!"

Yet try as he would, he couldn't find the street on the hill. He asked in the neighborhood, but no one had ever heard of the park with the fragrant trees. At last he said to Ninicchio, "What a fool I am! I must have fallen asleep on my feet and dreamed the whole thing." Then he laughed in spite of himself. "Tell me, Ninicchio, did you dream it too? What was the old man singing about?"

Winter came, with orange blossoms and rain, and then spring. Danilo's trees were covered with oranges. When children came to visit, Danilo would sing and tell them stories as he worked. Their favorite story was about the mysterious disappearing fruit.

"But you know," he said one day to Rosa, Caterina, and Filippo, "I don't need to sell magic fruit. Look at my orange trees! I'm a lucky man."

Danilo's cat blinked his big green eyes. He was listening to something else. Somewhere down the road a trembly voice was humming a *tarantella*.

Rosa had been playing on the pile of rocks. "Danilo," she said, "I've found a plum! May I eat it?"

"A plum? There are no plums here, Rosa."

The little girl held up the fruit for Danilo to see, and as she did, a wonderful fragrance filled the air.

Danilo's laugh rang out. "Eat the fruit, little one! Share it with your friends. May it bring you health and good fortune!"

They ate until nothing was left, not even a seed. But Danilo didn't care. He sang, clapping his hands, and they all danced the *tarantella*.

Some say the rain that fell that night was particularly warm. Some say the wind blew from the east and the west at the same time—and at sunrise the roosters danced! Danilo slept all night and didn't notice a thing.

And in fact, it was his cat who saw it first, growing out of the pile of rocks Danilo had dumped so many months before: a small tree, already covered with blue, pink, and purple fruit.

If you ever pass his way, I'm sure Danilo will give you some.